Miss Lilly
and
the Hollyhock
Garden

Written and Illustrated by
Mary A. Martin

For more information:

Website: www.kidsgardenspot.com

ISBN 1-58597-107-3

If you are unable to order this book from your local bookseller, you may order directly from website.
Quantity discounts for schools or other organizations are available.

To help get your hollyhock garden started, Lilly wants to give you a packet of hollyhock seeds FREE. All you have to do is send a stamped envelope with your name and address on it to:

Hollyhock Seeds
P. O. Box 12034, Parkville, MO 64152

Be sure to print clearly. Allow 4 to 6 weeks for delivery.

Printed in the United States

To my grandmother,
whose hollyhock garden
on her farm
filled many of my childhood summer days
with hours of
imagination and creativity
long before television
became the thing to do.

I hope her hollyhock people
inspire a new interest in
creating fun from something
as simple as a flower.

Hollyhock Garden was just north of the old farmhouse under the tall ash trees in the backyard. Wild plum bushes grew so thick you could not walk through them unless you were very small and very careful. In the spring, their small white blossoms made them look like one big white cloud. The fragrance was so wonderful that it was almost too much to breathe in and keep from floating away like a kite on the warm sweet air.

For the hollyhock people that didn't matter. They lived at the top of the hollyhock plants, above the big wavy leaves where the air was always the warmest, the sun shone the brightest and the bees were the busiest; and where Lilly, her family and her friends were the happiest.

Lilly, what a name! Lilly could never understand how she got that name. She was a little hollyhock lady, not a lily. But everyone called her Miss Lilly and that was all right.

Everyone in Hollyhock Garden was special in their own way. The girls looked pretty with their colorful bell-shaped blossom skirts and matching petal tops on their heads. The boys were very handsome with their wrapped petal pants and just as colorful petal tops. Every hollyhock family was a different color. No family was more beautiful than the other. Together they made Hollyhock Garden a sea of wonderful colors, filling the space between the fence and the road that ran by the old farmhouse.

Life in the garden was peaceful and happy. Every morning Lilly and her family would awake to the warm rays of the sun or the music of a gentle rain. All day Lilly would watch the birds flying by with twigs and feathers for their nest or bits of food for their babies. There was so much activity all around from the birds and the squirrels in the trees or the rabbits in the grass.

Lilly wished that she could go other places too. But how could she move from here? She was a flower blossom, and her place was to stay on the hollyhock plant. Still, she would dream of floating on the wind to wherever it would take her.

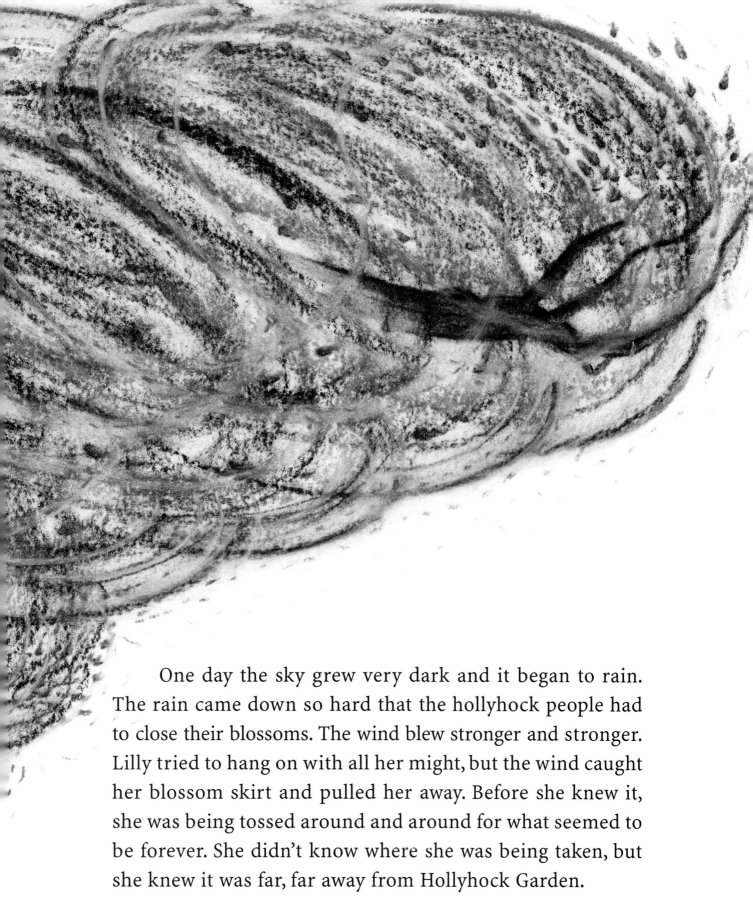

One day the sky grew very dark and it began to rain. The rain came down so hard that the hollyhock people had to close their blossoms. The wind blew stronger and stronger. Lilly tried to hang on with all her might, but the wind caught her blossom skirt and pulled her away. Before she knew it, she was being tossed around and around for what seemed to be forever. She didn't know where she was being taken, but she knew it was far, far away from Hollyhock Garden.

When the wind and rain finally stopped, Lilly landed with a soggy plop on the branch of a big oak tree. The sun came out again and slowly Lilly began to dry. She opened her petal skirt and looked around.

My, how different everything looks from clear up here, Lilly thought. This is nice and exciting, but how can I move from here?

Just then a robin landed on the branch next to her.

"Hello," said Lilly. "My name is Miss Lilly, and I live in Hollyhock Garden next to the old farmhouse."

"My name is Red," said the robin. "I do not know of any hollyhock garden or an old farmhouse. You must have traveled a long way from there. Would you like to come and stay with my family and me while you are here?"

Since Lilly had no place to go, she said yes and climbed on the robin's back. They flew a short way to another tree where Red and his family lived.

So this is what a nest looks like, Lilly thought. It was round and made with grass and twigs and lined with soft feathers. Two fat baby robins sat cuddled together in the middle. They opened their beaks and began to cry for food. The mother robin gave them each a small bug.

Lilly knew all the bugs that lived in Hollyhock Garden, but these sure looked different. She wondered why anyone would ever want to eat one.

This is nice, Lilly thought, but after living in a nest for six days, the baby robins were getting so big there was no room for her. She wondered out loud, "How can I move from here?"

Just then a grey squirrel came hurrying across the branch.

"Hello," said Lilly. "My name is Miss Lilly, and I live in Hollyhock Garden next to the old farmhouse."

"My name is Sara," said the squirrel. "I do not know of any hollyhock garden or an old farmhouse. You must have

traveled a long way from there. I am in a very big hurry to get home to my children. My house is much bigger than the robin's nest. Would you like to come and stay with me?"

Lilly said yes and climbed on Sara's back, holding tight to her fur.

Sara dashed down the tree, darted across a very large area of freshly mowed grass and ran up a huge white oak tree. Halfway to the top she stopped, looked around and slipped into a hole in the tree. Inside, it was big and warm with a table and four chairs, a cupboard full of acorns and a soft carpet of moss on the floor. Three baby squirrels came running to greet them.

"Mama, mama," they cried, "who is she?" they said together when they saw Lilly.

"She is our new friend," said Mama Sara. "She has traveled from a place far away and has no place to stay, so she is going to stay with us."

The three little squirrels crowded close to Lilly and introduced themselves.

"My name is Toby," said one.

"And, my name is Thimble," said another.

"My name is Little Miss Bitafur," said the smallest squirrel. "You know, bit-of-fur," she explained. "Mama named me that because I am so small, but I am very fast and my brothers can never catch me. It is important to be fast when you are a squirrel, isn't it?"

Lilly agreed that it was important, and Little Miss Bitafur smiled all over as if to say she was happy to be who she was.

Mama Sara announced that supper was ready, and they all sat down to eat acorn pudding and sip dewdrop tea. Lilly apologized for not eating any acorn pudding, but it is something that flowers cannot do. However, she said that she was very thirsty and that the dewdrop tea was delicious.

Days with the squirrels were filled with much activity. There was always something to do or somewhere to go.

Mama Sara was in a hurry to get more acorns collected and stored for the coming winter. Lilly, Toby, Thimble and Little Miss Bitafur kept busy with games and stories. The little

squirrels loved to hear about Hollyhock Garden and about the big wind that came and took Lilly to a faraway place. They agreed that when they grew big they wanted to go to Hollyhock Garden where the flowers were a sea of wonderful colors and everyone was beautiful and special in their own way.

All this talk of Hollyhock Garden made Lilly sad. That night as she lay on her bed of soft moss and felt the oak tree swaying in the wind, she remembered how nice it was to be with her family at the top of their hollyhock plant, where the air was the warmest, the sun shone the brightest, and the bees were the busiest. So the next morning, Lilly told the squirrels that she wanted to try to find her way back to Hollyhock Garden. Even though she was very happy with them, she missed her family.

"But how will you move from here?" asked Toby. "You always ride on Mama's back wherever we go."

They were standing outside on the branch of the white oak tree thinking about this when suddenly a strong wind came swishing through the leaves. It was so strong that it blew Lilly right off the branch, and she went falling towards the ground.

Then, something surprising happened! Lilly's petal skirt filled with the wind and floated her just like a kite. Lilly was amazed! She swooped and did pirouettes and dives on the wind. The squirrels all laughed and waved goodbye to Lilly as she floated off in the direction she thought she had come from.

All went well until the sun began to go down and the
wind stopped blowing.

Lilly landed softly on the ground. It was almost dark and she did not know where she was.

"Without the wind, how do I move from here?" she said out loud.

Hippety hop, a rabbit came hopping past Lilly in a very big hurry.

"Hello," said Lilly. "My name is Miss Lilly, and I live in Hollyhock Garden by the old farmhouse, and I am lost. Can you help me?" The rabbit went a bit farther and then stopped.

"Alright," she said, "you can come with me, but you can't stay long."

Lilly did not ask why, but quickly climbed on the rabbit's back and held on tight.

It was getting dark as the rabbit dashed across a field of tall grass. There were many fireflies darting about and stars shining in the sky to light the way. It wasn't long before the

rabbit slipped down a long hole in the ground to a burrow filled with little bunnies. They were jumping and playing, and there were so many of them that Lilly had to stay in a corner so as not to be stepped on by the happy little rabbits.

"Now do you see why you can't stay here for long," asked Mama Rabbit. "I just don't have room for anyone else, but you can stay for the night."

In the morning, Mama Rabbit took Lilly to the field of tall grass and hurried off to find food for herself and her babies. All alone, Lilly stood there again wondering how she could move from there. The wind was not blowing so she could not float like a kite. She was feeling very sad and

wondered if she was ever going to see Hollyhock Garden and
her family again. She was so sad that she started to cry.

"Can I help you?" said a voice above her. Lilly stopped crying
and looked up. Sitting on a blade of tall grass was a very
large and beautiful admiral butterfly.

Lilly began to explain all that had happened, the big wind that carried her away, the robins that helped her, Mama Sara and Toby, Thimble and Little Miss Bitafur, and now Mama Rabbit. But what was she going to do now, and how was she ever going to get back to Hollyhock Garden?

"I know where the old farmhouse and Hollyhock Garden is. It really is the happiest garden I have ever seen, with the most wonderful sea of color and where everyone is beautiful and special in their own way. I can take you there if you like," said the butterfly.

"Oh, yes!" cried Lilly happily.

The butterfly picked Lilly up, and away they flew towards Hollyhock Garden.

When Lilly and the butterfly arrived at Hollyhock Garden, everyone was happy to see her and anxious to hear about her great adventure.

She told them about the scary ride on the big wind that took her away, and how she landed on the big oak tree. She told about the robins and living in their nest. She told them all about Mama Sara, Thimble, Toby and Little Miss Bitafur, and how Mama Rabbit had so many babies that she could not stay there.

Lilly said she thought she would never see Hollyhock Garden and her family and friends ever again until she met the admiral butterfly, and he knew where the garden was.

The next morning, as Lilly sat at the top of the hollyhock plant, where the air was the warmest, the sun shone the brightest, and the bees were the busiest, she was very happy. Now she knew that if she ever wanted to move from there she could. She had many friends who would help her. Besides, way up high on a hollyhock plant is just the right place to catch the wind and float like a kite on the warm sweet air.

Planting Your Hollyhock Garden

1. In the spring, after all danger of frost has past, choose a sunny spot for your garden and clear any debris. Have mom or dad help loosen the soil by spading or raking. (The soil is best spaded in the fall so it can settle over the winter, but can be done in the spring.)

2. Once the soil is ready, scatter the seeds letting them fall into the small crevices made by the rake.

3. Next you will need to press the seeds into the soil. Your bare feet are perfect for this. But, if the weather is still cool, you should wear some old shoes.

4. Once you have carefully pressed down the garden area, you will need to water the seeds very well with a misting spray from your garden hose.

The seeds will come up in 10 to 14 days. As the seedlings grow, you will need to water each day or whenever the soil gets dry. The adult plants need 18 inches of space between each of them, so you will have to remove some of the seedlings if all the seeds sprout and come up.

You can plant your hollyhocks with other flowers. Since they are so tall, plant them in a row or group them behind the other flowers.

How To Make Your Hollyhock Dolls

      Start by picking the fresh, single-petal open blossoms. Double-petal blossoms do not work as well. Each should have a 1/4- to 1/2-inch stem. Pick a firm, plump bud of the same color for each of the blossoms. The bud should be open just enough to show the petal color at the top. Now you are ready!

1. Take a bud and carefully remove all the green bud casing by pulling each section downward and tear off at the base of the bud. You will now see the small holes created where the petals and the base of the bud come together. Two of these holes will be the eyes for your doll.

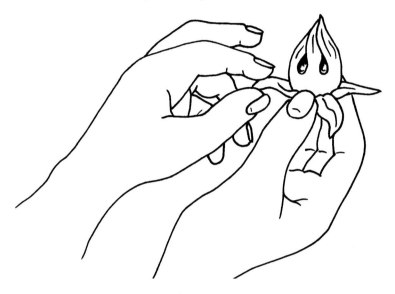

2. Next, remove the small stem from the base of the bud. A thumbnail works great for this, or have mom or dad cut if off with a knife.

3. Take the matching blossom and push its stem into one of the holes in the bud. Your flower doll is now complete. Repeat for all the picked blossoms.

To make a boy doll, pick a bud that is almost ready to open but the full-sized blossom petals are still wrapped shut. Attach a bud head the same as you did for the (girl) open-blossom dolls.

Be creative! Mix head and body colors. Choose almost-open buds for heads to make queen dolls or other characters. Tiny and medium-sized buds can pe put together for baby dolls. *Most of all, have fun and know each doll is beautiful in its own way!*

To help get your hollyhock garden started, Lilly wants to give you a packet of hollyhock seeds FREE. All you have to do is send a stamped envelope with your name and address on it to:

Hollyhock Seeds
P. O. Box 12034, Parkville, MO 64152

Be sure to print clearly. Allow 4 to 6 weeks for delivery.